This Little Tiger book belongs to:

_____

_____

_____

For Joel,
Charlie and Seth
~ J C

LITTLE TIGER PRESS
1 The Coda Centre, 189 Munster Road, London SW6 6AW
www.littletiger.co.uk

First published in Great Britain 2015
This edition published 2016

Text and illustrations copyright © Jane Chapman 2015
Visit Jane Chapman at www.ChapmanandWarnes.com
Jane Chapman has asserted her right to be identified as the author and
illustrator of this work under the Copyright, Designs and Patents Act, 1988

A CIP catalogue record for this book is available from the British Library

Printed in China
LTP/1400/1373/0915
2 4 6 8 10 9 7 5 3 1

JANE CHAPMAN

No MORE CUDDLES!

LITTLE TIGER PRESS
London

Barry lived by himself deep in the forest.
He liked strolling about on his own, listening
to the birds and tasting juicy berries.
But Barry was **never** on his own for long . . .

It was the same
thing **every** morning.
Before you could say:
"Huggle-wuggles . . ."

"Fluffikins, we missed you!"

"Hey! It's Cuddle Monster!"

"Hurray! Snuggles
is here!"

...Barry was **smothered** in **cuddles.**

Barry liked cuddling, **of course he did.**
But he was fed up with being smoothed
and stroked, and fuzzed and fluffed

all the time.

"I just want to be **alone**," he sighed.
"I know. I'll make a disguise,
so no one will know it's me!"

But Barry's disguise **didn't work** at all.

"Maybe if I was a bit more scary?"
he wondered.

So he put on an **angry** face and growled,

"GRRRRRRRRRR!"

"Oh, poor Cuddle Monster!" said Badger.
"Are you a bit **grumpy** today?"

"Hey, everyone! Barry needs a shnuggle-buggle!"

Barry groaned. The cuddles had to STOP!

So he painted a **huge** sign.

WANTED: comforting creature for cosy cuddles. Could this be YOU?

Lots of animals wanted the job.
But none of them were
quite right.

"Too teeny!"

"Too spiky!"

"Too
stinky!"

Barry was about to give up,
when at last he saw . . .

...the fluffiest snuggle-pops **EVER!**

Bear was **perfect!**
His tummy was snuggly.
His fur was silky.
And his hug was
just right.

Barry was delighted.

**"Bunnies,
badger,
beaver!"**

he called.

**"Anyone want
a cuddle?"**

"Me!"

"Me! Me!
I want a cuddle!"
the animals cried.
Big and small, they
rushed as fast as they
could towards Bear . . .

. . . and **zoomed** straight past him!
"What are you doing?" cried Barry.
"Don't cuddle me –

cuddle Bear!"

But it was too late.
The animals threw
themselves at Barry.

Barry wibbled.
He wobbled. Then he
toppled right over . . .

SPLAT!

... straight into a **swamp**.
The swamp was
oozy-squoozy,
mucky and yucky.

The animals looked at Barry in **horror**.

"Where has all the fluffy gone?"
they cried.

"It's not snuggly at all!"

One by one the animals
hopped off to get clean . . .

... leaving Barry all by himself.
"No more cuddles for me,"
he grinned. "Well, not for a little while anyway!"
Then he wiggled his huge toes, smiled
his **enormous** smile and squelched
down happily into the mud.
Peace at last!

More brilliant books to enjoy with **your** little **cuddle monsters!**